Budulienko and Pinocchio Tale

Jozef J. Matejka

First published 2016
by Rowanvale Books Ltd
Imperial House
Trade Street Lane
Cardiff
CF10 5DT
www.rowanvalebooks.com

A CIP catalogue record for this book is available from the British Library.
ISBN: 978-1-911240-44-0

The visit

Around the globe we chased the sun,
looking for a better life and for some fun,
until we arrived at the little island of Malta.
Not too far away from home, you can even lie
in the sun and tan.
This is the place where our story truly began.

You know what they say, the more the merrier.
This was true for our small island,
as many good people, from different places,
foreign countries, and even different races,
crossed our paths and created wonderful
memories,
as new friendships formed, in the
Mediterranean breeze.

One fine day, my daughter came home from
work,
and she brought along her new colleague,
together with her daughter, who always had a
naughty grin.
Our new South African friends they have
become,
Tatum, the playful little girl and her mum.

A few weeks later, they paid us another visit.
As we were talking, I noticed that Tatum
started to fidget.
I could tell she was bored and wanted to play,
being a child once, I understood, and a story I
started to relay.
Coincidentally, a few days back, I had
published my story book.
I liked Tatum, so I let her have a little look.
She quickly became lost in the story about a
little boy,
Budulienko, and to his adventures she listened
with joy.

She always held her breath until the very end.
Every time we met, an hour story telling I
would spend.
As I read the story, she almost remembered
every single rhyme.
She always cried and begged to hear it one
more time.

And so it was, one fine day, we all set out,
to Sicily, to see its wonders, without a doubt.
The beautiful Taormina, one of the most
picturesque cities.
I was inspired by its magic and wrote a few
ditties.
In the distance, the majestic Etna stands,

in all her glory, respect she demands.
I sat on the terrace, drinking wine,
looking out at the calm, turquoise sea, so fine.
For a second I stopped to think:
is this real, or is it just a dream?

The romantic main street in Taormina,
boasts a wide array of gift shops.
Any mementos or souvenirs your heart
desires,
this street is a paradise for any buyers!
As we passed all the colourful shop windows,
I couldn't fail to notice the little wooden boy,
whom every shop sold, as a children's toy.
Almost a symbol for Italy. As naughty as they
get,
Pinocchio, the wooden boy we met.

Carlo Collodi would be proud if he knew,
what a wonderful story he gave to so many
children.
It didn't take long, I soon found myself telling
the story to Tatum.
Soon after, we stopped at a small corner shop
nearby,
to buy the wooden toy, you know how
children are.

As a storyteller, I enjoyed seeing Tatum's

interest,
she was only four, so lost in the story she
didn't even want to rest.
It has always been so, since the day the Earth
first existed,
that the children in our world were and still
are truly gifted,
for their untouched souls can see past a
materialistic life.

For a child, a story is a portal to a land full of
excitement and joy,
before they close their eyes and fall asleep,
holding onto their toys.
The parents silently creep out of their
bedrooms and put away the storybook.
And before they leave the room, at their little
angels sleeping, they look.

After our Sicilian adventure had come to an
end,
we got one last visit, from our new South
African friends.
Tatum and her mum came to say goodbye.
As we were chatting away, Tatum let out a
sigh.
She stopped to look at me, I could tell she was
a little shy.
And then she asked me an unexpected

question, I won't lie.
"Are Pinocchio and Budulienko friends?"
I started to stutter, she caught me off guard,
but I realised that this is an author's time to
play his best card.
Tatum inspired me and got my imagination
running wild.
"Yes, they were best friends." I smiled.

Once upon a time...
"They don't start stories like that," Tatum
stopped me.
She was right. In today's world, full of robots
and superheroes,
nobody wants to hear a story without guns
and explosions.
I might be older, however I still understand,
but "Once upon a time" is how the story
began.
It might not even be so much a story, as a
rhymed recollection,
of the adventures and journeys of two little
boys.
So sit tight, gather all your toys,
our story is starting- don't make a noise.

Everything is going to be as it truly happened,
as well as how it was meant to be.
Don't be scared, let your worries leave,

your own imagination will help you believe.
Listen closely, you're about to find out,
the answer to your question, there's no need
to pout!

We all know when Pinocchio was "born",
the day when Geppetto, his father, no longer
had to mourn.
The day that he cut out a little wooden boy
from a tree trunk,
the one who grew up to be quite a hunk.

On the other hand, nobody really knows,
when, for the first time, Budulienko saw the
light of day,
but I think it's fairly safe to say,
that it must have been sometime close,
as these two grew up to be the best of
friends, never foes.

It's important to add that Pinocchio is Italian,
and rather loud,
while Budulienko is living in Bratislava and can
be too proud.
This means that they couldn't have met
before they were destined to meet.
But as you well know, in a story like this,
nobody gets old.
So they had plenty of time as from country to

country they strolled.

An unforeseen encounter

An exhibition of children's illustrations is held
in Bratislava every other year.
Few of its kind exist worldwide, so the Slovaks
hold it very dear.
What can be more beautiful than illustrating
books which bring children so much joy?
Seeing the excitement on their faces, they
want to see more, not a bit coy,
as they look in awe at the beauty of the
pictures in their books,
whether princesses, unicorns, or of pirates
and crooks.
It is a hard job to take on, turning those
frowns upside down.
But sometimes all it takes is a prince on a

white horse, or a queen with a crown.
And so, we came one step closer to the first
time,
that Budulienko and Pinocchio met.

On an Italian television channel a programme
was aired,
previewing the Slovak exhibition, as thousands
of children at their TVs stared.
Beautiful pictures full of colour caught every
child's attention.
Not even Pinocchio was spared from being
amazed.
He quickly packed his bags, and to Slovakia he
raced.
He could afford, so all his money he did count,
and after all, children get a discount!

It didn't take long until he found himself right
in the centre of all that beauty;
he even got free sweets, because he's a cutie.
Quietly he stood and gaped in awe as a boy,
similar in age, stood close by,
laughing and making fun of Pinocchio. He
caught his eye.

"Hey, you! Why are you laughing?" Pinocchio
shouted at the other boy.
"You never saw an Italian before? Stop

laughing and being rude,
it wouldn't hurt you to be a little coy!"
The other boy didn't seem taken aback.
"Sorry, my friend, I didn't mean to offend, it
often happens to me,
that I can't stop laughing at something I
happen to see.
And today it happened to be you, and the way
you gaped quietly,
but I apologise. Tell you what, why don't we
go and get some tea?"

"Oh, I'm sorry, I'm being rude again,
as I forgot to introduce myself. My name is
Budulienko.
I come from around here. And just like you,
I wanted to visit the exhibition and see the
beauty, too!
I took a look at you and I immediately knew,
as I saw you waiting outside in the queue,
that you and me are more alike than meets
the eye.
So I thought I'd find a way to come and say hi.
For you and me both have been around a long
time,
making children laugh and smile with our
adventures and stories."

"So, you're from far away?" Budulienko

continued talking.
"You really came all the way from Italy? But enough of that,
I'm sure we will have plenty of time to discuss.
We should carry on with the exhibition, it's getting very late.
If you want, you're more than welcome, now that we have finally met,
to be my friend and maybe join me on my next adventure."
Pinocchio's face lit up. "Sure! I like making friends and you seem pretty all right."
They shook hands and walked off into the night.

As they walked side by side, Budulienko started thinking,
"Do you have somewhere to sleep tonight? It's still quite cold outside."
Pinocchio didn't seem like he had it well thought out.
He quickly nodded his head without a sign of doubt.
"You can sleep at ours. I'm sure my mum won't mind!
We take care of our friends and always try to be kind."

This is how their wonderful friendship had

begun;
new adventures and never-ending fun.
But let's not skip ahead, we still have a story
to say,
so let's start right now, on the very next day.
But first, one thing still needs to be explained.
How is it that an Italian and a Slovak can
understand each other?
It's quite simple actually, because in their
fairy-tale world,
no matter from what country they are, they
understand each and every word.
A special language, created with the right
amount of love and a hint of magic,
spoken especially by the famous fairy tale
clique,
a language called Metoyoutome. It is very
unique.

Budulienko lived in a rather large house. He
had lots of space and a pet mouse.
He showed Pinocchio to the guest room
where he would spend the night.
But first, they had a dinner to attend to, under
the moonlight.
As everyone knows, after midnight, all the
toys come to life,
and gather together, all over the world, to
keep close to each other they strive,

at least for an hour, each day, till the clock hits
one. Then they must go back to sleep,
till the next day, when they hear the clock's
midnight beep.
This is how it works in the magic world, they,
too, deserve rest.
After all, they make children laugh, they do
their best.

The next day, as soon as the boys woke up,
they rushed for breakfast, and two hot
chocolate cups.
Budulienko's mum greeted them with a wide
smile
and served them their pancakes in a large,
delicious pile.
Just as every other mum, she very well knew,
how fast her little boy and his friend could
chew.
So she made another batch of her pancakes
with honey,
and when they were done, she gave her son
some pocket money.

Pinocchio was still a little shy as he thanked
Budulienko's mum,
for letting him stay the night and feeding him
so well.
She smiled, as she was used to her son

bringing home new friends.
He didn't like to be alone, he always needed a partner in crime.
Together they would play and the apple trees in the garden they would climb.
His mum understood and enjoyed seeing her son happy.
He was still her little baby. She even remembered changing his nappy!

In the afternoon, the boys returned to the city one more time,
to see the rest of the exhibition. They didn't even need to pay a dime!
Everyone knew who they were and was very kind.
When you come from the fairy tale world, a helping hand is not hard to find.
Budulienko showed Pinocchio almost all of the city.
They saw all the important sites apart from a few churches, what a pity.
The boys got on so well that, soon, weeks had flown by,
always together, they just couldn't say bye.

The journey

One fine morning, after having breakfast,
Budulienko's mum had some time to spare,
so she sat down by the boys on her favourite
chair.
"You know what, boys? I think you are both
getting a little bored,
as the whole city by now you have toured.
I just got a call from Grandma, it seems like
she is rather lonely,
and I thought it would be a good idea, if only,
you could visit her up in the mountains.
You can show Pinocchio the wooden cabins!
I'm sure Grandma will love to have you boys
up there,

she has never seen an Italian, and she is
missing you.
You will take her some food and make her
happy too!"

She knew they were two big boys
who no longer needed to play with toys.
The journey wasn't long and the path was
straight,
and if the weather got bad, they could stop
and wait.
She would arrange for someone to meet them
halfway,
just to make sure that the boys wouldn't stray.

The boys were happy that they were
entrusted with this task.
They quickly packed, and prepared some fresh
tea in a flask.
Budulienko's mum was thoughtful and quickly
started baking,
even though after a long day her back was
aching.
She packed all the goodies in a wooden
basket,
telling the boys not to eat any before they
arrive,
after all, she had counted them, there were
five.

Pinocchio stared in amazement, as if he'd read these words before.
"Well, of course! Little Red Riding Hood, we all know what she wore!
Her red riding hood, made by her gran,
before a big bad wolf tried to play a cruel trick.
Thankfully, she escaped, as the wolf wasn't too slick."
What if it were to happen to them too?
Thankfully, rumour had it the wolf was resting at home,
as he had come down with the flu.

"However, another threat lurks out there in the forest,
big and dangerous, one of the brownest."
Budulienko's mum tried to scare the boys.
"I will surely be relieved when I'll know you made it there alive,
if you meet a bear, it's unlikely you'll survive!"
The boys became white with fear,
and they almost let out a tear.
"Come on, boys, you know it's just a bit of a tease,
in the forest you can walk with ease.
The path is safe, away from all the bears,
you will only see a few birds and maybe some hares."

"My two heroes, I know you will be just fine,
you will travel in the sunshine.
It's true, you always must be careful, no
matter where you go,
in this world you don't know who's a friend or
a foe.
But Budulienko knows the way well,
and all the neighbours are kind, your fears you
can dispel.
I didn't mean to frighten you so much,
I only wanted to teach you a lesson as such.
Come on now, we've spoken enough,
you need to get some rest, and finish packing
your stuff."
She gave them one more hug goodnight,
as they all left the kitchen, and switched off
the light.

The next morning, as soon as the boys woke
up,
they were both excited to get on their way.
They double-checked all their bags,
and made sure they'd put on the correct
address tags.

They drove down to the railway station,
and checked the platform from where the
train departs.
They soon heard the train conductor's whistle,

which meant it was time to get on the train.
The weather turned out great, no chance of
rain.
"Keep in touch and take good care,
of any dangers, always beware.
I love you both, enjoy your trip!"
Mother waved goodbye to them,
as the train made its way towards the
mountains.

Once the boys got off the train, they were met
with a surprise.
Their aunt and her daughters were happily
waving,
the boys couldn't believe their eyes!
They immediately exchanged hugs and kisses,
as Budulienko admitted that his family he
often misses.

The boys couldn't help but blush,
as everything went down in such a rush.
They weren't expecting to meet two such
pretty girls.
They are gentlemen, but they both like girls
with curls!
They must have been close in age
and Pinocchio, in true Mediterranean fashion,
was about to introduce the boys with Italian
passion.

But before he had a chance to speak,
the girls gave them a kiss on the cheek,
and quickly said there was no need for
introductions,
because they very well knew who the boys
were,
they read some of their stories on the way
there in the car.
"My name is Michaela and this is my younger
sister, Sarah,
we were looking forward to meeting you,
we hope you are excited to have some fun
too."

It didn't take long before the girls were
begging their mum,
to let them go up to the mountain to play with
the boys sometime.
It was not too far, after all they live down in
the village,
and it was only a few minutes to get to
Grandma's cottage.

The trip didn't take too long, they even sang a
road trip song,
as they made their way up the mountain in a
horse-drawn carriage.
The road was rough and they had to hold on
to their baggage.

As they turned the last corner, a wonderful
meadow opened up,
blown away with amazement, Pinocchio
almost dropped his cap.
In the middle of the meadow they could
already see,
a humble wooden cottage, a hare, a doe and
even a bee.
Beautiful silence surrounded the sunlit
meadow,
heaven on earth, where only wonderful things
grew.
When the dark fell, the fairies came out to
play,
they celebrated and danced until they saw the
light of day.

And so, in front of her wooden cottage,
Grandma was happily standing.
She was eagerly awaiting her beloved
grandchild,
outspoken, clever, witty and sometimes a bit
too wild.
But she always gave him all she had, after all
he was her favourite one,
even though he made her mad sometimes,
she still loved him a ton.
As the boys got off the carriage and collected
all their stuff,

they said goodbye to the girls and tried to act
buff.
They knew this was no goodbye but a 'see you
soon',
as they had agreed to meet sometime under
the old plum tree.

"My dearest boys, I have prepared something
delicious for you,
let me go fetch it quickly, I won't be long,
with sweet homemade treats you can never
go wrong!"
As Grandma left, a thought came to
Pinocchio's mind.
"Don't you think it's rather odd, that your gran
is so kind,
her eyes aren't wide, her pupils don't enlarge,
her ears aren't big, her nose isn't large,
she doesn't have fangs,
and under her dress, no tail hangs?
She doesn't seem to be the mad old wolf,
who wears robes and likes to scam,
could it be, because she really is your gran?"
The boys started laughing, it's an age-old joke,
they like to tease little Red about her gran,
and her red silk cloak.

Grandma took good care of the boys,
she fed them plenty and even bought them

toys.

But the boys knew what they had to do,
they always worked when their chores were
due.

They took care of the cottage and cleaned up
the stable,
and when it was dinnertime, they laid the
table.

A dangerous decision

Grandma didn't want the boys to work too
hard,
they were there to have fun and play in the
yard.
They came from the busy streets of a big city,
where there was not much fresh air, what a
pity!
One fine day, the boys ventured into the
toolshed,
Grandma forbade them to play there, but they
forgot what she said.
They made up their mind to gather some
firewood,
to put in the fireplace, it would be good.
The evenings did get rather cold,
and the heat also helped to keep away the
mould.

They quickly noticed a set of axes lying on the
ground,
an opportunity to execute their plan they had
found.
They weren't too heavy, they could easily lift
them up,
so they agreed to compete; whoever chopped

the most wood.
"One, two, three, GO!" As side by side they
stood.
They were feeling like two lumberjacks, big
and strong,
joking around. What could go wrong?
They had almost chopped up all the pile,
when suddenly Pinocchio found himself lying
face-down,
with his foot right under the swinging axe.
Would Budulienko be so vile?
Pinocchio quickly screamed for his friend to
stop.
"Budulienko, it's my foot! Don't chop!"
Budulienko's face filled with fear,
and a second felt as long as a year.
Budulienko quickly let go and started to cry.
Pinocchio got up and wiped the tear from his
eye.

When both of the boys calmed down and the
shock had passed,
they came back to their senses pretty fast.
They both knew how serious this accident
could have been,
Budulienko almost chopped his friend through
the shin.
Budulienko was so caught up in the
woodchopping,

he didn't realise that Pinocchio's wooden leg
he was gripping.
He grabbed it by accident when he reached
for another piece of wood,
luckily Pinocchio yelled as loudly as he could.

Budulienko apologised for the mistake, he
would never harm his friend.
Then they shook hands and gave each other a
hug, all was well at the end.
This was a lesson they had learnt forever,
what they did, was not very clever.
They agreed not to tell Grandma about this
ordeal,
they both knew how worried it would make
her feel.

How the boys took the goat to graze

One fine day, Grandma asked the boys for a
favour,
if only they could walk the old goat 'Mica' and
graze her.
She told them which part of the forest to go
to,
but the boys were too excited and they said
they knew.
She sent them close to the old brick plant,
the goat can graze with ease, the ground
there doesn't slant.
A place where the earth is as red as the bricks
that it used to produce,
but nobody remembers, as the factory has
long been in disuse.
"There will be other boys too, I'm sure you
will get along,
enjoy yourselves and don't be too long."

The boys set off together with the goat,
keeping in mind to watch out for the moat.
They secretly packed beanshooters and
slingshots,
surely the other boys would have them too.

They don't do much harm, it only stings a bit,
and leaves a small mark wherever you get hit.
The parents knew that there was no need to
worry,
their children were safe, out of danger's harm,
the most that could happen was a small
scratch on the arm.

There were around ten boys in all,
most of them heard the mountain call.
Some came to play, others preferred to sit and
watch.
They soon split into the small groups,
for Cops and Robbers. Each team assembled
its troops.
This is where the first disagreements began,
not everyone was happy with their clan.
Everyone wanted to be a robber,
but without the cops there would be no game,
you need at least two teams, or so was the
aim.
The boys assumed their positions.
The robbers hid all over the place,
on the word GO, they started the race.
The rules were simple, if you were shot you
were out,
and if you were a sore loser, you couldn't
pout.
When your friend was also shot and now

there were two of you,
you could play a new game or wait for a new
turn.

It was hot under the burning sun,
the boys often needed to cool down after
they'd run.
A stream wound around the old brick plant,
they often went for a dip,
there was no one around to tell them that
they couldn't.
The stream also served as a good setting,
to shoot their friends on the other side, with
their slings.
They assumed their positions yet again,
and so the game all over began.

As you could expect, they soon forgot all
about the goat,
they thought she would be close by, chewing
oats.
There were no wolves or bears in sight,
so they quickly returned to their imaginary
fight.
Suddenly their game was interrupted by a
helpless bleating.
The boys turned to look, only to be met by a
sad scene.
The goat wasn't grazing where she had been.

But she had wandered off towards the
gushing stream.
To take a few sips, she'd tried to balance on a
wooden beam,
but the wood was wet and she must have
slipped.
By the time the boys came to her help,
she was so tired she could barely yelp.
She was sinking deeper and deeper into the
muddy stream's bed,
the boys came in the nick of time, the water
was already up to her head.

It wasn't as easy as it might have looked,
the boys too were sinking, the power of the
stream they had to brook.
They were all very scared of getting punished.
For a miracle to happen they all wished.
Thankfully, their wish soon came true,
the mud was no longer holding onto the goat
like glue.
Four boys each freed one of the goat's
hooves,
and with joint effort, lifted her up to a nearby
plain,
but this time they decided it was better to tie
her up with a chain.

However, one small problem still remained,

what would be the excuse for the goat being
mud-stained?
The boys were clever, they knew they
wouldn't get away with a lie,
the goat must be cleaned, they at least had to
try.
And so they had to walk for an hour or two,
to a close by river whose waters they knew,
calm enough to let them stand on the edge of
the moat,
and collect some water to wash their dirty
goat.
They washed all the sticky mud away,
to see her coat's whiteness in the light of day.
They even laughed and cracked a few jokes,
about a dirty goat being washed by a few
blokes.
They did get rather wet themselves,
but this surely wouldn't get them in trouble.
They could always say they stepped in a
puddle,
and in case their mums still got mad,
they would surely get the support of their
dads.

When Budulienko and Pinocchio arrived
home,
Grandma asked them where they went to
roam.

She thought the goat was rather tense,
but running after two boys all day, it made
sense.
The goat's udder was full, she must have fed
well,
so about the mud on her legs, Grandma didn't
dwell.
Grandma got slightly cross with how dirty the
boys were,
they also had mud in their hair.
Grandma was just about to ask what they had
been up to,
when Pinocchio quickly cut her off,
"Well you know how it goes, we were playing
a game,
when suddenly one of us fell in the stream,
Jozef was his name.
It was an accident, so there is no need to
throw around blame.
We quickly ran to help him out, he didn't even
need to shout.
Needless to say, we got a little wet and
muddy,
but, oh well, what wouldn't you do for a
buddy!"

Grandma laughed and didn't even notice,
how Pinocchio's nose suddenly grew longer.
Her love for these two boys each day grew

stronger.
Deep down she suspected it wasn't the truth,
but what can you do with the modern youth?
After all, a white lie never hurt anyone.
They're good boys who just want to have fun.
She prepared a good supper to warm them
up,
she even made hot chocolate, but they were
allowed only one cup.
The boys were so tired that they went straight
to bed,
they could barely see, their eyes were so red!

Never bored, in the forest there was always
something to do,
like run outside and feel the fresh morning
dew.
They spent all the days playing outside,
or their bicycles they liked to ride.
Sometimes they would clean the barn,
and pretend that they owned the farm.
In the evening they always came home to a
good treat,
Grandma liked to bake and the boys liked to
eat!

The river raft races

You could often see the boys playing by the
riverbend,
pretending to be fishermen, they didn't want
the fun to end.
Everyone knew that in this river there were no
fish,
so instead they used to catch toads and frogs,
and would use them to scare the villagers'
dogs.
The water here was crystal clear,
the animals would often come and drink,
fox, hare, bear and even deer.

However, the thing they liked to do the most,
was to race their wooden rafts down the river.
From nearby rocks they built a racing track,
they worked hard, they didn't slack.
They carved their rafts out of the best wood
they could find,
they weren't experts, but they didn't mind.
They tried to carve each raft in a different
style,
the possibilities were endless, it made them
smile.

Once the rafts were ready, they placed them
at the starting line,
they counted to three, sometimes, as a joke,
even up to nine.
Once they released them, they watched with
joy
till their rafts reached the finish buoy.
They would run by the river, all the way,
to make sure that their rafts didn't stray.
At the finishing line, some were happy, some
were sad.
If they lost, they wondered if their designs
were bad.
They would take the raft home and see how it
could be improved.
They would test its speed, and the way it
moved.
At the end of the day, they were all good
friends.
It doesn't matter who wins when the day
ends.

Kites and notes

One early morning, as soon as they opened
their eyes,
the boys started to think of how to entertain
themselves.
"Budulienko, can you hear that? It seems like
there's a bit of a breeze.
Why don't we fly kites somewhere where
there are no trees?
The wind is good, the sun is up, we should get
them to fly with ease!
It's not spring yet, but that doesn't mean we
can't fly a kite.
Maybe we'll even call the others to join in and
play till the night.

You know what? There's something else we
can do.
We can send secret messages by kite too!
All you have to do is attach your secret note,
the kite will do the rest,
the kite will fly it high up to the sky, and
deliver it wherever you request."

They ate their breakfast and rushed to the
toolshed,
to collect all the equipment: scissors, wood, a
blanket and some thread.
They knew what to do, this wasn't their first
time,
it barely took a few minutes and their kites
were prime.
They kissed Grandma goodbye and said they
wouldn't be long,
they also asked if she would like to come
along.
She said she'd stay at home to rest and read a
book,
and later on, dinner she'd cook.

Soon you could see two kites flying in the sky,
competing over which gets more high.
It's not as easy as with the river rafts,
as it depends on the speed and direction of
the draught.

The kites were running wild,
like the imagination of every child.
A dragon flying high in the sky,
strong, courageous and spry.

It's not so easy to tame those wild beasts,
you need years of experience and skill.
But most importantly you need patience and a
strong will.
Sometimes a kite would snap in two or the
string would tear,
in which case another kite with your friends
you'd have to share.

As the kites were gliding on the summer
breeze,
the boys decided it was time to send their
secret messages.
They each took a piece of paper and wrote
whatever was on their mind,
maybe someone out there, their messages
would find.
They slit their papers a little bit from the side,
and made sure that to the kite they were
properly tied.
A problem only arose if a kite fell down.
That's why they didn't fly them close to town,
for someone might find their secret messages
before they did.

Therefore, once a kite fell, they ran as fast as
they could,
to reach their fallen dragon first, before the
rest of the boys would,
so usually it was better to not write anything
too cringeworthy,
for they would all find out, and you would no
longer be perky.
And so, even this time, the boys ran for their
lives,
as they tried to find their fallen kites.
Budulienko came across Pinocchio's kite first.
As he realised, into a teasing laugh he burst.
He quickly grabbed the secret message,
and was tempted to read out loud a short
passage.
"Budulienko, please! We're like brothers,
I would never read your message in front of
the others!"
It didn't take much for Budulienko to feel bad,
after all he'd never want to make his best
friend sad.
He handed the piece of paper over to him,
but he took his chance, even though it was
slim.
"I gave you the paper back, although I'd still
like to know
who the message was for, I promise I won't
make a show."

Pinocchio thought for a bit and came up with
the right thing to say:
"Nothing special, Budulienko. I only wrote that
I had a lovely day!"
Before he even finished his sentence, his
wooden nose began to grow,
which meant that he had lied, as you all well
know.

"It's not very nice to lie to your friend,
after all the time that we together spend.
Unless you tell me the truth now,
the soil for a week you'll have to plough!"
Budulienko exclaimed.
"Forgive me Budulienko, my dearest friend,
I didn't mean for the fun to end.
I was just a little too shy,
and I thought you would make me cry,
if I told you about the wish that I wrote on my
note.
The truth is that it is about Michaela and
Sarah,
and how I'd like to get together with them and
play.
You know, I think about them every day."
Pinocchio admitted.

Budulienko couldn't help but laugh,
about Pinocchio's supposed gaffe.

"Do you know that I wrote about it too?" he said.

"I was thinking about it last night in bed.
I wonder if there's a way we can get in touch with the girls,
maybe we can meet them, and give them some fresh water pearls."
The boys were embarrassed that they didn't trust each other enough,
to open up about how they felt instead of acting tough.
They walked home and discussed it along the way
and laughed about the adventures of their day.

After they cleaned up and ate their dinner, they quickly found themselves in bed.
They were quite tired, but there was another reason too,
Grandma promised to tell them a story if she had nothing else to do.
They weren't classic fairy tales, the kind they've heard a million times,
but they were her own true stories, no thought-out rhymes,
the type that made you wonder, and want to know more,
you could listen for hours, they'd never bore.

Grandma's scary stories

The boys' favourite bedtime stories were the
scary kind,
even though some courage they first had to
find.
They would often be too scared and they'd
curl up under the quilt.
Grandma had to admit, she liked to scare
them and didn't feel any guilt.
They always begged her to tell them one
more,
even though from all the talking her throat
was sore.

So, even today, like every other day,
a new story she had prepared.
She spoke about how she used to pluck
feathers,
as when she was young, they used to fill quilts
with them,
and maybe even use them to decorate their
skirt's hem.
It wasn't the easiest of things to do,
and would often need an entire crew.
It might be a bit hard for you to understand,
but that's no reason for our story to end.

"Back in those days, almost everyone had cows,
fresh milk and good meat for every house.
Sometimes, however, it did happen, that a cow's milk ran dry,
and at every feather-plucking when they got together,
to find a solution or a new remedy they'd try.
As they plucked feathers, one by one,
their mouths worked faster than their hands.
They would gossip, laugh and talk about their weekend plans."

"Oh ladies, have you heard the latest news?
The reason why Anna has the blues?
Her cow's ran dry, she has no more milk.
And now she's afraid she will have to sell all her silk!
But listen on, there's even more!
I hear that it was her neighbour, Dora.
Apparently she went to town to ask for a witch's help,
and she had to pay by gathering some rare magical kelp.
The witch said a spell, which enchanted a frog,
that would appear at the first sign of evening's fog.
The frog would find the cows and suck all their milk,

only to disappear at first sign of morning light.
It happened so fast, the cows couldn't even
put up a fight!"

By this time, all the women were feeling
scared,
to go home alone in the dark, none of them
dared.
"And did you hear that John saw a ghost last
night?
He appeared out of nowhere and gave him a
fright!
Poor guy, he was still very scared today,
I asked him what he saw, but he wouldn't say.
At least he was lucky, because it happened
close to his home,
the only place, where uninvited ghosts can't
roam."

They continued to scare each other for a
while,
until they plucked an entire pile.
Soon they realised it was time to say
goodnight,
pack their bags, and hug each other tight.
They would wait for their husbands to come
for them,
as most of them lived quite far.
Back in those days, nobody yet had a car.

Sometimes if their husbands got sick,
someone else would have to walk them home,
often the kind mountain sheriff, Rick.

"Okay, my dear boys, that's enough for today,
it's time to switch off the light.
Close your eyes, surrender to the night.
I hope you don't believe all the silly things I've
said,
don't keep thinking about it while you're in
bed.
It's time to sleep, no need to feel scared,
but before you sleep, some nice tea for you I
have prepared."
They kissed each other goodnight and
Grandma left the room.
The boys couldn't help but feel a bit of gloom.
They covered themselves all the way up to
their eyes
for they were scared, and you all know,
that under the bed, the monster lies.
Grandma left her door slightly ajar,
so she could hear if they called for her from
afar.

So it was, their worst nightmare came true.
They woke up halfway through the night,
to a strange thudding sound that gave them a
fright.

As if someone was hastily stomping around
the room,
huffing and puffing, not minding the gloom.
They felt helpless and didn't know what to do,
what had entered their room they had no
clue.
The strange noise kept coming close.
They couldn't move, with fear they froze.
Calling for Grandma was their last resort,
the monster's evil plan to thwart.

"Grandma, please rescue us, come quick!
To beat the monster, bring your broomstick!"
The boys kept on pleading for help.
From her room Grandma could hear them
yelp.
She quickly ran into their room,
switched on the light and swung around her
broom.
She was quite surprised with what she saw,
two terrified boys with a juddering jaw.
"My dear boys, where is your monster?
Can't you see that it's just a confused
hedgehog?"
She was right, for they could see,
a lost little animal which was trying to flee.

Grandma walked to the door and opened it
wide,

and told the boys there's no need to hide.
The hedgehog quickly found his way out,
he was as scared as the boys, without a doubt.

"Didn't I tell you to close the front door?
A hedgehog came in, but it could have been a
wild boar!
Serves you right, your lesson you have learnt,
when you play with fire, you get burnt."
Grandma laughed and tucked them back into
bed,
and gave them a kiss on their sleepy heads.
The boys couldn't fall asleep again,
they realised they weren't yet men.
Still young, they were only boys,
no more scary stories if they still play with
toys.

Grazing geese

The next day, early in the morning,
the postman brought Grandma a letter.
She put on her glasses, read it over twice:
the town shop was selling discounted rice.
Grandma didn't have a lot of money to spare,
how she spent it she had to beware.
"My dear boys, I will go down to the city,
you can't come with me, what a pity.
But if you'd like, you can walk me down,
and wait for me in the village while I go to
town."
The boys saw an opportunity, a chance they
couldn't miss.
They agreed with their grandma and gave her
a kiss.
Soon, they were busy setting up a plan, finally,
to meet the girls if they could.
It seems that their secret wish came true, the
one they wrote on the kites they flew.

Grandma prepared some delicious snacks and
packed them in separate sacks.
It wasn't long before the boys found
themselves knocking on the girls' door,
and hoping that they wouldn't be in the

middle of a chore.

Their mum opened the door with a smile on her face,

"Hello, boys, you're at the right place!

My girls haven't stopped talking about meeting you.

They were a bit bored, they had nothing to do.

They were begging me to let them walk up to your home,

but in the forest, I didn't want them to roam."

The girls were excited, even happier than the boys.

Their mum knew that guests always have to be fed,

so she sent Michaela and Budulienko to fetch a fresh loaf of bread.

In the meantime, Pinocchio and Sarah helped her lay the table,

and then she asked them to bring fresh milk from the dairy.

They had almost finished eating, when their mum exclaimed,

"Oh no! I almost forgot about the geese!

I have to go and feed them, but first I'll eat my last piece."

"Don't worry, we'll do it," Pinocchio said.

"We'll make sure the geese are well fed."

You could soon see four children followed by a
dozen geese.
They had them under control and walked
them with ease.
They all had their feathers shining bright
white,
especially in the strong noon sunlight.
Only the gander had some colour around his
neck.
He seemed to be angry, Pinocchio he tried to
peck.
They didn't have to walk too far,
after all, close to the meadows they were.

They walked for some time, till they found the
perfect spot,
to throw a picnic, since lots of snacks they'd
got.
First they chatted and joked around,
till some much-needed courage they all found.
The girls weaved dandelion wreaths,
as the boys scouted a few cherry trees nearby,
to pick some cherries they wanted to try.
The boys were soon climbing the trees,
having fun, careless and free.
When they thought they had collected
enough,

they climbed back down, which was a bit
more tough.
Afterwards, they basked in the sun.
They quickly fell asleep after having so much
fun.

In about an hour or two, Budulienko awoke,
Pinocchio he tried to prod, "Wake up, this
isn't a joke!"
Unfortunately, he said it a bit too loudly.
Soon, four sets of eyes were looking round.
It didn't take much time for them to notice,
that the geese had disappeared.
They didn't know where they were,
or if they were all right.
They went in twos to search around,
but only a few loose feathers they found.
Was it a wolf, perhaps a bear?
We know that geese, they like to scare.
"Come on now, let's all calm down and walk
back home,
there's nothing else to do, we've done all that
we could."

The girls' mum knew something was wrong,
she realised; they had taken so long.
She also saw their sad faces and not even one
goose in tow,
she feared this would happen, but how could

she know?
"What happened, my children, where are the
geese?
Were they blown away by this light summer
breeze?"
Right on cue, as if they had it planned out,
the six o'clock broadcast started to talk about,
how twelve geese were found wandering
alone,
and are being kept safe on the town council's
lawn.
It also said that the owner should come
straight away,
that he has to pay a fine and some interest
per day.

When the shock and panic faded away,
the children could enjoy the rest of their day.
But this time they stayed away from the
geese,
they were thankful they were still in one
piece!

The sun slowly started to set, it was getting
late,
they knew they'd soon see Grandma at the
gate.
In fact she soon arrived, and asked the boys to
pack their things,

she even brought the girls a gift, sweet silver
rings.
One should have seen the begging that
ensued,
the boys were both almost in tears,
thankfully, Grandma was all ears.
She heard them out, and knew it was only fair,
the boys could stay if the girls had some more
time to spare.
They all agreed and Grandma rushed home
before the dark set in.
When she thought about the boys, she
couldn't help but grin.
After all, every parent knows what it's like,
whether the kids want a puppy or a new bike.

How Budulienko and Pinocchio scared themselves

So they stayed over for that night.
They promised to be good and not start a fight.
They tried to be mature, born gentlemen,
they had to impress the girls, that was the plan.
As their mum watched them happily chat away,
she would never guess what they'd invent the next day.
In a small town like this, word travels fast,
but luckily, it doesn't last.

The boys from the village knew Michaela and Sarah very well,
the prettiest girls around, everyone could tell.
With the presence of our two heroes the village boys weren't very pleased.
The girls didn't even notice that Budulienko and Pinocchio were being teased.
"What are you going to do, you big-city boys?
You think that you own the world?
At least, us villagers, we don't play with silly toys.

And you over there, you're like a wooden
plank,
you think you can impress with your Italian
swank?"

The girls quickly shushed the village boys.
"Is this one of your immature ploys?"
The girls defended our heroes, they promised
to be on their side,
true friendship is rare, you must defend it with
pride.
However, Budulienko and Pinocchio wouldn't
go down without a fight,
they had a revenge fully planned by the end of
the night.
Together with the girls, they prepared an
elaborate plan,
to bring havoc into the village boys' clan.

The next day was a sad day for the entire
town,
you could tell, everybody wore a frown.
A beloved woman passed away that week,
a funeral was being held by the creek.
She was very chipper, always kind,
some time to talk she would always find.
She collected herbs, and made special teas,
if you were feeling sick she would cure you
with ease.

Needless to say, people assumed she was a witch,
she didn't work, but you could tell she was rich.
So, they thought she would use her hocus-pocus,
some magic herbs and dried locust,
maybe even a short witchy spell,
to grant her every wish at the ring of a bell.
Even on this day, as they all gathered before the sermon,
people were gossiping and trying to speculate,
about how she had met her fate,
and how strange things happened in her presence.
It was hard enough for the adults to hear,
let alone for the children who were shivering with fear.
This time also happened to be Budulienko's and Pinocchio's chance,
to execute their plan, in the gloomy setting their aim was enhanced.
Pinocchio stood on Budulienko's shoulders,
and the girls threw a blanket over them.
Once they found their balance, Pinocchio grabbed a wooden stick,
and they slowly made their way down the street,

where the village boys had stopped to eat.

You wouldn't believe the panic that followed.
Everything which had legs ran away.
The village boys went to hide in a nearby stack
of hay,
while all the girls and women desperately
screamed,
"The ghost of the old witch!" Or so it seemed.

Our two boys found themselves standing in
the dark street all alone,
they didn't mean to cause such panic, if only
they had known.
They looked around, left and right, they
couldn't see a single soul.
Fear overcame them, they were scared, each
other they had to console.
They quickly realised that what they did was
not a funny joke.
They didn't mean to scare all the town folk.

The girls were waiting for them round the
corner,
as that was what they had agreed, before they
carried out the deed.
The girls quickly realised why the boys were
white with fear,
after all, they did just make a ghost appear.

The girls grabbed them by their hands,
and ran all the way to the safety of their
home.
It took a while for the boys to calm down,
but even so, they couldn't help but frown.
The girls made them fresh mint tea,
"Revenge never pays, you see!"
The boys just smirked and looked at each
other.
"We had to teach them a lesson, what would
you rather?"
They decided it was better to call it a day,
and anyway they were too tired to play.

The next day, the ghost's appearance was the
talk of the town,
as well as how the village boys were falling
down,
as they jumped over a fence, trying to flee,
and eventually hid behind a tree.
People also spoke of how the women
screamed,
many ended up with no voice, their
neighbours deemed.
Some people watched the panic pass from
behind their windows.
Whether they laughed at least a bit, nobody
knows.
Thankfully, nobody found out that our two

boys devised this master-plan,
they were all convinced they really saw the
ghost of their neighbour, Anne.

How Pinocchio became the town hero

During breakfast on the next day,
they were discussing what they could play,
for it was the last day of their stay,
before they must get on their way.

They had almost finished their breakfast
when, suddenly,
they heard loud cries from the street, but
most importantly,
the cry was followed by a sound of galloping
horses.
One could also hear shouting by various
voices.

They quickly ran out onto the street,
where a horrible sight they would meet.
A herd of horses had got spooked,
and were now running towards the
playground.
To run into the children there, they were
bound.

Pinocchio quickly evaluated the situation,
he started running without a sign of
hesitation.
He jumped into the middle of the road,
the horses saw him, their gallop slowed.
He took advantage of their lower speed,
to try to stop their crazy stampede.
He grabbed onto the horses' manes,
and steered them into the other lane.
He held on tight, whispered soothing words in
their ears,
the people already started to cheer.
And so the horses slowed down and
eventually came to a stop,
Pinocchio prevented a tragedy and saved the
day,
when he kept the children out of harm's way.

Pinocchio quickly became the new town hero,
he worked his way up from a zero.
"You know, us cool guys do this kind of thing

every day,
stopping horses, and even giant monsters we
can slay!"
Budulienko laughed and joked.
However, his proudest moment came soon
after,
when in between all that laughter,
a village boy came to speak to him,
and asked to make amends, hiding a shy grin.
He also asked for forgiveness for making fun
of them,
he admired them both and wanted to make
friends.

Obviously, Michaela and Sarah, too, were
impressed,
they knew that their favourite boys were the
best!
They showered Pinocchio with hugs and
kisses.
Pinocchio appreciated this more than any
riches.
Budulienko felt proud of his new brother,
he knew it from day one, there is no other.
He told everyone they were best friends,
and that his hero services he recommends.
The time flew by much too quick,
they were happy, that must have done the
trick.

It was time to go back to Grandma's cottage,
to keep her company for a few more days.
It was hard for them to say goodbye,
the girls both wanted to cry,
but they are ladies, they must try,
they put on brave faces and wiped their eyes.
"This isn't goodbye, but a 'see you soon',
never forget, we live under the same moon.
We're never too far to meet again!"
And so they were all left with wonderful memories,
as they walked their separate ways in the summer breeze.

Once they arrived back home, the boys didn't waste any time,
they were eager to tell Grandma about their adventures.
She listened to them and was happy that all went well,
even though she was feeling down about their impending farewell.

A quick farewell

They spent their last few days together,
even though they passed by in a whirl.
Before they knew it, they heard a knock on
the door,
they weren't surprised, they knew what it was
for.
Budulienko's mum came to pick them up,
and even though they were sad that their
time was almost at the end,
some time with Budulienko's mum they were
looking forward to spend.

"My children, I'm sorry to come and interrupt
your fun,

but every good thing must come to end.
Budulienko, my son, it's time to return to the city,
and Pinocchio must go back to Italy, I know it's a pity.
His friends have called me more than once
and asked me to deliver him a message,
that so long without him, they cannot manage.
They miss him too, just like I've missed you,
without you I didn't know what to do.
When you love someone and they're not around,
the world stops turning, the sun is nowhere to be found."

The boys thanked Grandma for all she had done,
they were well-fed, warm, loved and they also had fun.
They promised they would come back as often as they could.
This time they couldn't fight back the tears,
not even Grandma, despite all her years.

They said many goodbyes, and the hardest one,
was for the boys to say bye to each other, but it had to be done.

At the airport, they tried to be brave,
they hugged tightly and did their best not to
cave.
Sadness filled their hearts,
that the time had come to part.
They promised each other that this adventure
they'd never forget,
they learnt new lessons, laughed, and were
left with no regret.

So, this is how Budulienko in Pinocchio found
a lifelong friend,
and how our exciting story must finally end.
But now, dear Tatum, it's time to go to bed,
so that Pinocchio and Budulienko can meet
again,
while you dream, in your sweet little head.

Explanations

- **Biennial of Illustration Bratislava (BIB)**
  - one of the oldest international honours
  for children's book illustrators. Artists
  are selected by an international jury,
  and their original artwork is exhibited
  in Bratislava, Slovakia.

- **Bratislava** – capital city of Slovakia

- **Budulienko** – a boy from a classical Czech
  folktale

- **Carlo Collodi (1826 – 1890)** – an Italian
  children's writer known for the world-re-
  nowned fairy tale novel *The Adventures of
  Pinocchio*

- **Etna** – an active volcano in Sicily, Italy

- **Pinocchio** – a wooden boy from the fairy
  tale novel *The Adventures of Pinocchio*

Author Profile

Jozef Ján Matejka was born on the 10th of March, 1949, in Trenčin, Slovakia. A doctor by profession, he started taking an interest in poetry during his college studies. However, he only became serious about writing in 2000, when he moved with his family to Malta. There, he wrote and later published his first book, a poetry collection called Príležitostné Básne. Matejka has since authored six books, over the course of which he worked with two Slovak painters and a photographer, who helped him with the illustrations.

Publisher Information

Rowanvale Books provides publishing services to independent authors, writers and poets all over the globe. We deliver a personal, honest and efficient service that allows authors to see their work published, while remaining in control of the process and retaining their creativity. By making publishing services available to authors in a cost-effective and ethical way, we at Rowanvale Books hope to ensure that the local, national and international community benefits from a steady stream of good quality literature.

For more information about us, our authors or our publications, please get in touch.

www.rowanvalebooks.com
info@rowanvalebooks.com

Lightning Source UK Ltd.
Milton Keynes UK
UKOW07f1104091117
312452UK00008B/39/P